Listen

"It is good to love many things, for therein lies the true strength, and whosoever loves much performs much, and can accomplish much, and what is done in love is well done."

—Vincent Van Gogh

Listen

Holly M. McGhee

ILLUSTRATED BY Pascal Lemaître

ROARING BROOK PRESS • NEW YORK

Listen

to the sound of your feet—
the sound of
all of us
and the sound of me.

Look

to the shining sun.
It is for you
and all of us—
it is for me.

The stars—

they are for you
and all of us.
They are for me.

Breathe.

Smell the air.
My air is yours and all of ours,
your air is mine.

Taste.

The food you eat
is also the sun
is also the rain.

The food I eat
is also the sun
is also the rain.

Dig

in the earth.
Your roots are mine,
my roots are yours,
the roots of all of us
are the same.

Yet you are you and I am me and we are we.
Us . . .

Listen
with your heart.

It is
your ears
your eyes
your nose
your mouth
your hands.

Your heart
can hear everything,
see everything,
smell everything,
taste everything,
touch everything . . .

Your heart can hold everything.

Including the world—
its darkness and its light.

Including your story,
including my story—
including the story
of all of us . . .

And when your heart hears your own story,
it hears my story too.

Your story
my story
our story . . .

Listen

to the sound of your feet,
the sound of all of us,
and the sound of me.

For Jeanne and Bill Steig,
who taught us about
the freedom of lines and words
and the strength of love
—Holly & Pascal

Published by Roaring Brook Press
Roaring Brook Press is a division of Holtzbrinck Publishing Holdings Limited Partnership
120 Broadway, New York, NY 10271

mackids.com

Library of Congress Control Number 2019930860

ISBN 978-1-250-31812-1

Our books may be purchased in bulk for promotional, educational, or business use. Please contact your local bookseller or the Macmillan Corporate and Premium Sales Department at (800) 221-7945 ext. 5442 or by email at MacmillanSpecialMarkets@macmillan.com.

First edition, 2019
Designed by Elizabeth H. Clark

Printed in China by RR Donnelley Asia Printing Solutions Ltd., Dongguan City, Guangdong Province

1   3   5   7   9   10   8   6   4   2